7 Mór dark tales

7 Mór dark tales

Christine Grace

Illustrated by Wendy Straw

A B R O L L Y B O O K

Dedication

This book is dedicated to my beautiful family,

Charlie, Ollie and Hannah Rose.

— *Christine Grace*

Brolly Books
(an imprint of Borghesi and Adam Publishers Pty Ltd)
Suite 330, 45 Glenferrie Road, Malvern Australia 3145
www.brollybooks.com
email: emma@brollybooks.com

First published in 2019.

Text by Christine Grace.
Illustrations by Wendy Straw.
Cover design by Wendy Straw and Emma Borghesi.
Internal page design and book specifications by Emma Borghesi.

Printed in China
ISBN 9780648457152 hb
9780648457183 pb

Publisher's Note

7 Mór Dark Tales is written in prose poetry form,
with a focus on imagery and rhythm.
Therefore, conventional grammar rules have not been applied
where to do so would disturb the poetic effect.

A catalogue record for this
book is available from the
National Library of Australia

 Contents

Moving against the tide

It is the silence that wakes him, and he swims to the window to look outside. But she is not there. He is uneasy, remembering the great storm in the night. He wonders if his daughter is lost in it.

Sending his servants out, word comes back that she was seen, beyond the far reefs, carrying a young man.

'Moving towards the land,' the servant whispers, and the King is struck with dread, although he hides it.

'No matter, no matter,' he mutters, swimming from the throne room out into the garden. His other daughters are playing and singing. Except for his eldest daughter, who watches him.

Diving down to his youngest daughter's bedroom, he is looking for a sign. Behind the mirror, under the bed, behind the wardrobe.

But he finds nothing.

Taking his supper in the tower room, he is seeing the passing kingfish on the tide. Their silver, blue backs catching the sea light.

Yet the sight gives the King no pleasure.

And his eldest daughter, from the outside of the window, is watching him again.

'Where is she?' he asks of her.

She is silent, as always, but her eyes are knowing.

'Has she been captured? There was a ship, I know, broken in the night. The servants say there are dead sailors in the sand. Tell me, Daughter, has she been captured?'

She swims away and the King plunges through the window, following her, their great tails lifting and falling, lifting and falling. Although worrying for his youngest, the quiet presence of his eldest calms him.

Together, father and daughter rise to the shallows where the setting sun casts its last light.

The King now remembering her birth. She came out of her mother, so easily, that her mother slept on.

The moment just before, the King had woken. He had lifted the bed cover. The Queen's swollen belly was softly pushing. Then she had come, his eldest, with no cry at her own arrival but a wondrous look upon her face. Floating up to him, the King had caught her. And still his wife slept on.

'A babe born in the bed?' the wet nurse whispered upon her arrival.

Her eyes were wide-eyed and magical.

'No cry, Your Majesty, no discomfort to the Queen?' And the King had nodded and together they had gazed at his eldest child, now asleep in her royal cot.

And yet still his wife slept on.

From then on, she was a constant, silent presence in his life. For no words had ever come to her, nor song. She was there at the birth of her many sisters, hovering just behind as his wife struggled in her child labours.

Her first daughter had been easy but the rest of their children caused her great pain. The birth of their youngest daughter was his wife's undoing, and after she was born the Queen had lain back upon the bed, exhausted. A year on, she died.

It was he alone that had carried the Queen's body, down to the graveyard. But his eldest had followed.

Together they buried her, their great tails swishing in the sand, digging a hole so deep no fish or sea creature would ever find her.

The servants say there are dead sailors on the land.

Whilst he wept by his wife's graveside, his daughter had swept the sea floor into strange and beautiful patterns. And it was as if the sea had stopped breathing, the water was so still.

The patterns had lain there for hours and little fish and bigger fish had come. They could be seen staring at the enormous and wondrous thing that she had made.

Even in his grief, the King had marvelled. Where had she come from, his strange and silent child?

Now, together, searching for his youngest, they dive deeper. She leads him over the desert sands where nothing lives. There is the newly broken ship.

They swim past the bodies of the dead sailors, whose strange legs move about on the lower tide, as if they were dancing. And their arms move up and down, and the King is again uneasy.

Has she been captured? Has she been captured?

For three days they swim until he can see, far ahead a figure coming towards them. He knows it is her, his youngest, returning.

She swims by. Their presence is nothing to her.

The King is struck cold by her indifference. Then his rage erupts, from all the worry of the past few days. Thrusting his tail, speeding through the water he seizes her and shakes her, cursing her for being thoughtless and cruel.

And her eyes say nothing.
And her mouth says nothing.

The King, ranting and raving, finally releases her. Turning, she swims homeward, as if untouched by his outburst.

Back at the palace the King, furious, swims to her bedroom. She is lying in her bed, seemingly asleep, with her bed cover pulled tight around her.

He pulls the cover back and shouts, 'Get up, get up!'

'You get up!' she shouts back, and she hits out, her hand knocking his crown off his head and it goes flying into a corner of the room. It spins round and around, and the King, watching it, is shocked and shaken. When he turns back, she is gone.

In the morning, the King wakes and he thinks it must have all been a bad dream. He lies in his bed waiting for his youngest to come and sing to him by his window, as she has always done. She has the finest voice of all his daughters and the songs she sings make him laugh.

But she does not come.

Enraged, he flings open the door to her bedroom and shouts into the empty room, startling the little fish behind the curtain. No-one has seen her.

The King, used to his own way, goes to the witch. He wants her to make a potion for his youngest, so that she will do as she is told.

But the witch is not there.

The King thrusts his tail, swimming to the rocky outcrop and then back again to the golden gate.

Up and down, up and down, gnashing and grinding

his teeth. He orders his servants, a thousand of them, to fetch the great anchor. He orders another thousand to carry its chain.

And so the deed is done.

Dragged across the sea beds the anchor wreaks havoc, destroying the grounds of the breeding fishes. But the King is incensed.

And his youngest appears and shouts at him for the destruction that he has caused.

And he drags her by her hair and ties the heavy chain three times around her waist.

And so she is kept.

From his tower window, he is watching her.

She is silent, with her jaw jutting out. He's seeing how she's changed. As if a thief has come and stolen her away and before him is a stranger he does not know.

His eldest daughter is swimming out to her, carrying a golden plate. Full of abalone and oysters, freshly shucked and salted. She refuses to eat.

That night he cannot bear it. He swims to her and tries to speak to her kindly. Touching her arm, he tells her that he will unlock her if she promises to keep nearby.

Slumping over the chain, her hair is hanging down. The sea pushing her and pulling her, in all its little currents. As she lies, sad and listless.

And the King is reminded of the dancing dead sailors from the shipwreck. He feels insane, not

And he drags her by her hair and ties the heavy chain three times around her waist. And so she is kept.

knowing what is happening to his sweet serenader, she who makes him laugh.

He swims away and then back to her again and then away. Lost, not knowing what to do at all. How he's wishing that his wife were here to give him counsel.

And then he sees them. The deep cuts on her tail. Criss cross. Criss cross.

They are not cuts made from a careless brush across the coral. They are cuts, made with the sharpest knife.

Swimming to her room he finds it, wrapped up in kelp, behind her dresser. His eldest daughter has followed him.

'Have you seen what she has done?', and the King feels sick. She takes his arm and they swim back to

And the witch says even though he wears a crown he has no power.

his youngest. The eldest daughter rattles the chain.
The King is ashamed for all that has happened.
He releases his downcast daughter.

A healing balm is ordered. Her room is closed for
three days. The King swimming back and forth, back
and forth, waiting for his eldest and youngest
daughters to emerge.

On the fourth day, the King, diving down to the sea
garden, sees all his daughters. His youngest's hair
has been woven with sea flowers, into fish plaits.
Her pearl necklace softly glistens around her neck.
Although a little quiet, she seems content to be back
with all her sisters.

The King is pleased.

In the morning, waking, he looks to the window.
She is there. She looks at him in a way he has never seen
her look at him before.

An unease is stirring in him, but then she's singing. It
is such a silly song, about a dolphin who keeps sneezing,
that his laughter is drowning out his doubt and fear.

Later that day, he swims by her window and peeks
inside her room. And he is struck down.

On the floor she has carefully arranged sea shells into
words. They say, 'No more sea.'

Sending his servants out in search of her, he knows she
will not be found. She has gone.

He goes to the witch and she shows him his daughter's
tongue, cut out and given freely, for two legs. And the
witch says that even though he wears a crown he has no
power.

And the King knows that the witch is truth-telling.

That night, his eldest seeks him out. He's weeping
in the bed, so full of grief, so broken. Taking off his
heavy crown, she quietly strokes his head.

The King thinks how he orders his servants about.
To fetch his dinner, to hear him pontificate,
to shine his golden palace in the sea. And the servants
bow to him and do as they are told.

His crown lies on the bedside table. It was his father's
crown and his grandfather's crown before that.

And he's thinking that it's a paper hat because it's been
a trick upon his head, and that is all. 'Take me to her,'
he says to his eldest daughter. He's pushing back the
bed covers.

Together, they plunge through the window. They swim
for five days until the sea floor rises, following the
contours of the shallow reefs until they arrive at a
beach.

Together, their heads just break the surface. They
see a large party on the sand. Music plays loudly and
there are many young people, dancing on their strange
little legs.

The King sees her. His youngest, amongst them,
and she's moving to the music, her long hair
swaying to and fro. Moving on her legs to the rhythm,
but it is not easy. He is seeing that. Her face is
shadowed in pain.

Her two little legs step up and down, her strange little
toes gripping the sand, as if she, too, is fearful of
falling. In this new found land.

A young man comes, very handsome. Taking her arm, together they are dancing, their bodies pressing in on one another. His daughter is silent and smiling, through her pain.

And the King is now knowing that she lives in a foreigner's land. A place where he cannot visit, for there is no place for him there.

He watches her little feet stamping in the sand and the way she drinks from a bottle which seems to ease her pain. He cannot watch anymore. He cries, forlorn, into the water. What a mournful cry. A mournful cry, for a lost king and his daughter.

His eldest gently takes his arm. Together their tails move up and down, up and down, taking them home.

A year passes.

The tide moves in and the tide moves out.

Every day the King wakes and he looks to the window. It is an old habit that he finds hard to break. In his dreams she is singing songs that haunt him.

His other daughters play in the garden but their songs are subdued. They can feel the grief of their father and his distance to them.

His eldest daughter is watching him.

Three more years pass.

The tide moves in and the tide moves out.

His eldest comes to him, taking his arm.

Together their tails move up and down, up and down. He knows she is taking him back to the sandy beach, and even though he dreads it his tail keeps pushing him forward.

For he knows he is an empty shell who cannot feel the things around him. The words he is speaking are hollow. He is without connection or purpose.

They arrive at the beach. His eldest is beside him, leading him to just beyond the break, her long hair swirling in the foam.

There is a small child playing on the sand, putting water in its little bucket and taking it up further, pouring it out, watching it disappear. Then, on its little legs, it goes back to the water's edge and fills up the bucket again. Going back and forth, back and forth, entranced.

The King, surprising himself, sings a little of a lullaby he use to sing to all his daughters when they were little.

The child now runs to its mother, grasping at her legs as she stands in the sun's rays, her hand cupped over her eyes, looking out. It is she.

And the King sings a little more.

And the woman walks further into the water on her strange little legs. And the King sings a little more, louder and stronger.

She is smiling.

The King breaks out into a glorious song. Thrusting his tail, breaking through the surface.

With his arms stretching, arching his back, kicking again. Up, up, up, propelling himself, into the blue of the sky.

His eldest joins him and together they dive through the waves, shooting up into the air, their great tails splashing. The waves, rising and falling, rising and falling. They are beating the water and the foam is frothing more and more. Flying away on the light sea breeze.

She is waving to him.

It is a sweet, sweet song that fills the King's heart and he sings it out, loud and true, into the world. How he sings his song!

He catches a glimpse of his silent daughter on the sand. Her eyes are shining and they say to him back. 'I see you Father. I hear you.'

Diving through the foam he thrashes about, filled with such power and joy. Yelling and crying out. Singing more to his daughter on the sand.

The tide moves in and the tide moves out.

Every year he returns. Always with his eldest, sometimes with his other daughters. And each year he brings his youngest a new song.

Sometimes she stands alone by the water's edge, sometimes she has more children with her. Her hand, cupping over her eyes, the sea lapping at her feet.

And the light catches the shining scales of her family that she knows and loves.

Years pass.

The tide moves in and the tide moves out.

The King dreams. She is singing to him from the window and it is a lullaby. Waking he finds his eldest daughter. Together their tails move up and down, up and down, taking them back to the beach.

She is lying on a rock. Her long hair has turned grey. It hangs over her shoulders. She is barely breathing.

The King lovingly gathers her in his arms.

Her eyes are crinkling at the edges, sparkling when they see him. And the father, through his tears, quietly sings to his daughter.

Her breath is almost gone.

He gently slips her back into the water.

They all turn homeward.

She is buried next to her mother. The King silently watches his eldest swishing the sand. Into strange and beautiful patterns. And the little fish and the bigger fish are coming, looking on the marvellous thing that she has made.

Winter is over

It is an enormous bird, and the girl, terrified, hangs back against the wall.

'Come closer,' it whispers, 'and cover me.'
Despite herself, the girl inches forward.

The eyes of the bird, so very black, watch her, glistening, in the torch light. The air is like ice in the tunnel. Water seeps out from its walls. Far above, where the earth meets the sky, it is winter.

Here in the deep, it is musty, damp, cold. The bird is lying on its back. Almost double the size of the girl. Yet she reaches up, covering the bird with the blanket.

Then she grows bolder, tucking the blanket corners under the bird's wings. Tattered and torn the wings are, tattered and torn.

'Thank you,' the bird whispers, closing its eyes.

The girl, wondering if it is about to die, steps closer again. She can see the faint rising and falling, rising and falling, of its breast. She is amazed at herself.

Finding the almost frozen bird that morning,
she'd stolen the blanket from her soon-to-be bridal
chamber. Dragging it behind her, through the house
of the sleeping mole, she'd reached the back stairs
undiscovered.

Carrying the torchlight to guide her, she had
disappeared far below, back into the tunnels.

Turning a sharp left at the junction, for the second
time that day, she had come upon the bird.
The enormous bird. In the torchlight.

She stands a while longer, watching the rising and
falling as the bird lies sleeping.

Deep inside, the girl knows that both the mole and
the field mouse will be furious about the bird. She
decides to keep it secret.

The bird is lying on its back. Almost double the size of the girl.

It will be something that is hers, and hers alone.

Leaving the bird, the girl goes back through the dark passages, back to the home of the field mouse. The field mouse is waiting by the door.

She is much smaller than the girl and has to look up to speak to her.

'Tomorrow you will carry the sheets and the towels to the house of the mole and then that will be the end of it,' the field mouse says. 'Now come and eat your supper.'

The girl sits at the tiny table, her knees tucked up underneath her chin. The girl eats her supper.

The field mouse watches her and ponders the situation. There is no doubt the girl is a pretty little thing and the mole from the big house has been taken with her.

Whether the girl has been similarly taken by the mole does not concern the field mouse because she is a practical mouse and can see an opportunity when it comes her way. The girl will be company for the mole in his old age and when his time is up his house of luxury, with all his servants, will become his neighbours.

'The Field Mouse of the Manor' she will be called. And so the marriage has been arranged.

After supper, the field mouse sends the girl to bed. It is a tiny bed and the girl can only rest her top half on it.

The field mouse sleeps on the chair by the fire.

The following morning, the girl carries the sheets and the towels to the house of the mole.

'Don't be late,' the field mouse says. 'Don't be distracted and remember to smile when you see him. It's important he sees that you like him.'

The girl nods and the field mouse watches her disappear into the dark passageway, carrying the torch. As she passes the junction, so close to the hidden passage where the bird lies, the girl pauses. But she dare not stop. The mole will be waiting.

She arrives at the mole's house and he is there by the top step, holding the dim lamp.

With his poor eyesight he can just see her coming out from the passage, far below. Not much more than a young girl, with long hair and pale skin she is a pretty little thing, although a little boney and worn for her age.

But she will do. He will fatten her up with chicken and pork and perhaps try his luck with her. Maybe, just maybe, she will bear him a child.

'Come, come,' he says, gesturing to her. His voice is gruff, but he quickly softens it. He knows it will serve him well not to scare the child. She climbs the stairs.

'What do you bring today?'

She inches forward, holding out her offerings.
'Fresh linen, towels and a jug for the table.'
She quickly curtsies as she had been instructed to by the field mouse and this pleases the mole.

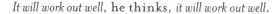

It will work out well, he thinks, *it will work out well.*

'Come, come,' he says again, and she follows him through the cook's kitchen into the Great Hall. He shuffles and shuffles and she keeps her distance from him, not too far for him to turn and whisper angrily, 'hurry up', and not too close for him to feel he is being hurried.

In this, too, the field mouse has instructed her.

Even though it is daytime, the mole keeps the house shutters tightly closed because the light hurts his eyes. Up the grand staircase they go and into the bridal chamber. A carved chest has been placed at the end of the enormous bed. Carried to the great house, from the home of the field mouse, three weeks passed.

'A glory box of sorts,' the field mouse had said,
*'full of pretty little things. Not things for your great house,
Mr. Mole, but young girls like such things.'*

The field mouse, being a practical mouse, had suggested that over a number of weeks the girl would carry various household items through the dark tunnels.

It will be a way of her getting to know you Mr. Mole,
the field mouse had said.
'It will be a way of getting her used to the idea.'

Thus far the plan had worked. Each day the mole meeting the girl on the back stairs and leading her through the great house, up to the bridal chamber.

'It is true that we are getting to know one another,' he tells the field mouse when she visits one morning to check on things.

Then he adds after a long moment,
'I believe we are developing a certain closeness.'

The field mouse had smiled and nodded as if she
knew that this would happen all along. But in her
mind she's wondering how long it will be before she
can ask for one of the mole's servants. She has a pile
of wood that needs cutting and she is tired of cutting
wood.

Now, in the bridal chamber, the mole puts the lamp
down and opens the lid of the glory box. In it the
girl carefully places the sheets and towels and the
little jug.

'Good, good,' the mole says.

The chest is now full. Every day since the marriage
was arranged the girl has walked the dark passages
between the two houses, carrying her offerings.
Six embroidered table cloths and a lace one for the
pantry.

'It will make the jam look pretty,' the field mouse had said,
'placed upon it so.'

Two butchers knives, seven face cloths with a large
'M' sewn on the left hand corners, a dinner set,
three large soup spoons, and a Chinese tea pot.

The mole drops the lid of the glory chest and it
bangs shut, making the girl jump a little.

'Good, good,' says the mole again and the girl knows
that, through his fur, he is watching her.

Behind him, she can see the door, connecting her
bridal chamber to his. She wonders what day it will

be opened, after they are wed. For, indeed, the field mouse has instructed her very well.

'Tell her about the bed,' the mole had scrawled on a crumpled note, handed to the field mouse last Wednesday. *'Tell her about the bed and what she must do,'* and the word 'must' had been underlined three times.

The field mouse had needed to sit down on her little stool, all rickety. The girl had felt that something important was about to be said. The field mouse, usually chatty, had gone so very, very quiet.

Now, standing in her bridal chamber with the mole the girl glances at her bridal bed.

It has been carefully re-made to conceal the theft of the blanket from underneath its cover.

She feels a new kind of feeling. One she has never felt before. She knows it has to do with the bird in the hidden passage and the blanket that covers it.

'We will have tea in the parlour,' says the mole.

The girl follows him back down the stairs, not too close and not too far. The parlour doors are already open and the mole goes in and the girl goes in, and he sits and then she sits and a servant comes and pours their tea.

The servant takes the lamp away.

The light, through the shuttered windows, casts a gloomy glow. The girl wonders about what it would be like to open them all and let the colours and smells and the sounds in from outside world, into this darkened room of the mole, who is soon to be her husband.

'Tomorrow bring the field mouse,' the mole says.
'There are the last of the preparations but then it will
be done and we will be married by the end of the week.'

She nods and then she sings to him a little, knowing
that he likes it when she sings.

Later that day, as she is walking back through the
passages, the girl wonders about the bird and whether
it's still breathing. But she is late and the field mouse
will be wondering where she is so she does not stop as
she passes the sharp left turn at the junction.

'What was he like today?' the field mouse asks as the
girl comes through the passage door and into the
kitchen.

'The same. I sang a little and did not get too close, nor
too far, when we were walking.'

The light, through the shuttered windows, casts a gloomy glow . . .

'Good,' says the field mouse. She looks at the boney girl and notices a slight flush in the girl's cheek.

The girl knows she is being watched so she says, 'He wants you to come tomorrow to finish the preparations.'

'Good,' says the field mouse again, slowly.

Something has happened to the child, but she is not exactly sure what.

The following morning, they take the torchlight and the field mouse has to scurry to keep up with the girl, so quickly does she walk through the dark passageways.

The field mouse thinks of the coming summer, after the snow has melted, when she can open her little doors and windows out into the fields above and let the sweet air in. How she longs for the winter to be over.

'Slowly, slowly,' she says as she scurries after the girl and the girl answers, 'he will be waiting and he does not like it when we are late.'

The field mouse is struck dumb as the girl has never answered her so, in such a fashion.

But she is right. The mole is waiting at the top of the stairs and is indeed bad-tempered. The field mouse thinks the girl is clever, to have known he would be irritable so she too hurries up the stairs, apologizing. No sense in upsetting him at such a time. The thought of a young wife at his age is enough to keep him on edge.

The girl is sent up to her bridal chamber. The field mouse and the mole have tea and they discuss the wedding plans and the reception and who will be coming and who will not and the cake and the wine and the music.

And all the while the field mouse is looking at the enormous house and the strange dark portraits upon the wall, and the golden jugs and the Persian carpets. And she thinks of the passages that lie between her little house and the mole's big house.

And then she thinks on the girl. The boney girl. And she wonders about the flush in the girl's cheek and her sharp retort when they were walking the passageway.

And the field mouse puts it all down to the note from last Wednesday, and what will be expected, when the bridal door is opened.

'He will not live for much longer' thinks the field mouse, *'and then I can live here with the girl and the servants and I might open up one or two shutters because it is indeed a gloomy place even though it is dripping in riches.'*

And as the mole is chatting on about who is coming to the wedding and how all his old friends are jealous of his young bride, the field mouse is thinking about which shutters she will open to let the light in. Then the field mouse is turning because the girl is standing in the doorway and it is unlike her to be there, and the field mouse is uneasy.

'What is it?'

'Is it not time to go back?' asks the girl.

The field mouse frowns and the mole looks angry because he has been interrupted. The field mouse is thinking she needs to say something very quick and clever to smooth things over.

'Yes, yes. Run along. Uncover the bread and put it in the oven, clever child. I forgot about it.'

And she smiles at the mole as if everything had been pre-arranged, as if the girl was meant to go without her, through the dark passageways.

Then she turns again and the girl is gone and the field mouse is again uneasy and she thinks how relieved she will be when the wedding is done.

She sits with the mole for the rest of the day and she wishes she could sing like the girl to shut him up because he is so tiresome.

When the field mouse gets back to her little house, the bread has just come out of the oven and the girl has the soup on the stove and she is quietly sewing. The uneasiness the field mouse has felt all afternoon leaves her.

The next morning, the field mouse wakes and the girl is gone. There is a cup missing from the table and a slice of bread has already been cut from the little loaf. The uneasiness of the day before comes back to her in an instant.

Just then, there is a knock at the door and she opens it and it is the mole. He walks right in, bending his big head and taking up most of the space in both the kitchen and the lounge and the field mouse knows she must be very, very careful.

'Where is she, the girl? Why did she leave yesterday?' asks the mole.

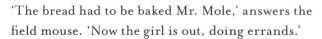

'The bread had to be baked Mr. Mole,' answers the
field mouse. 'Now the girl is out, doing errands.'

The field mouse says this firmly as she is a practical
field mouse and knows it is very important to give the
right impression.

The mole frowns.'She should be here when I come,'
he says.

'Let us go back together Mr. Mole. I will leave a note
for her to come when she gets back.'

So the field mouse leaves a note on the table saying
where they are. She's chatting to the mole all the way
through the dark passageways about all the things
that need doing when there is a wedding, and that
the girl is so very excited about everything.

Just before the junction, the mole stops and turns to the
field mouse, asking 'Do you think she likes me, truly?'

The field mouse is quick and says, 'Does she smile
when she sees you?', and the mole ponders this and then
he nods.

The field mouse places her little claw on his furry arm
and pats it saying, 'There you are.
A bride who smiles.'

They get to his house and the girl is waiting with the
lamp at the top of the stair and she smiles and curtsies
and the mole is so very happy to see her that everything
is forgotten.

But the field mouse is sure now, something is happening
to the girl because she does not know where the girl has
been and it is a dangerous thing, whatever it is.

The field mouse can't wait for the wedding to be done so she can go back to her little house and rest for a while.

The wedding takes place on the following Saturday. The mole's friends, all old and craggy, look bad-tempered as the mole and the girl are wed. But they drink plenty of mulled wine and dance with whomever they can find, even the servants and the stable boys.

They eat caviar and the mole has a spring in his step, that's for sure. While everyone is busy dancing and eating, the girl takes a torchlight and goes down the back stairs, carrying a little cup of water. She has sweet biscuits in her pocket.

At the junction in the passageway, she turns the sharp left and down a little way there is the bird, an enormous thing, lying underneath her stolen blanket.

'You will not be missed?' asks the bird.

The girl shakes her head, whispering, 'I am becoming very, very clever.'

'That is good,' says the bird.

She feeds him crumbs from her pocket and the bird tells her again of his family, where they have gone for the winter and how he had let them go because he had been caught in a thorn bush and had torn his beautiful feathers to shreds.

Out of her other pocket the girl takes a needle and thread and begins to sew the birds feathers back together with neat little cross-stitches. The bird is very grateful and tells her of the fields with the sweet, sweet corn and the marshes and the bracken, and the golden light and the green, green wood, and the girl sees everything in her mind as she is sewing.

After a while, she leans into him, completely unafraid, whispering, 'One day I will ride upon your back, Mr. Swallow, and we will go to those fields and the marshes and the bracken. The sweet air will be filled with blossom and honeydew and no more will I walk these dark passageways between the houses of the mole and the field mouse.'

Then she tells her one true friend about the door in her room, and the bridal bed and the note that was scribbled last Wednesday past.

The bird listens and his eyes are so very black, and he thinks on these things for a while.

'When the door opens, take the pillow in your bed, the biggest, most thickest of pillows, and place it where you have slept and go and stand behind the curtain until the mole has gone.'

The girl finishes her cross-stitch and cuts the thread very neatly, telling him she will do as he suggests.

Kissing her friend Mr. Swallow upon his feathered forehead, she tells him that she has never loved anyone until this moment. The enormous bird is quiet and warm and happy, and full of the sweet crumbs from her pocket.

Back at the wedding party, the mole and all his friends are asleep from drinking too much wine and are snoring on the sofas. The field mouse, a little tipsy, is chatting to the maid, when she sees the girl come in.

The girl smiles at her and curtsies, and the field mouse is momentarily put off guard, but then she sees the needle and thread, just peeking out from the girl's pocket. And the field mouse knows for sure that the girl has some strange and powerful secret, but she has drunk too much wine so she too lies upon the rug in the great hall, and falls fast asleep.

A week passes.

On the eighth night, the mole, rested from his wedding festivities, knocks on the door of the bridal chamber. He shuffle, shuffle, shuffles to the bed then, with difficulty, climbs upon it.

There he has his way with her. He is surprised at her softness and the way she yields to him and he is all the while thinking of his craggy old friends, and how jealous they will be when he can boast to them.

Then he kisses the girl gently on her cheek, but the room is so gloomy that perhaps it is her forehead, but it is no matter to him. He climbs off the bridal bed and shuffle, shuffle, shuffles, back to his bedroom, closing the door tight behind him.

Of course, the clever girl has done everything the bird had suggested, and is hiding behind the curtain. All she hears is a little whimper from the mole at some stage, and then the door clicking tight.

In the morning, the field mouse is at the big house having breakfast with the newly married couple.

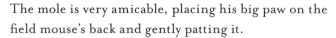

The mole is very amicable, placing his big paw on the field mouse's back and gently patting it.

Then he leans forward, whispering to her, 'She is not a girl anymore. Now she is a lady.' Then he winks and smiles and nods his head, giggling a little.

The field mouse looks across at the girl quietly eating, knowing the mole has had his way with her. But the girl seems well enough.

Then the field mouse wonders about the needle and thread. The girl starts singing, and the mole is finally quiet, so the field mouse turns to the shuttered windows and thinks once more upon which ones she'll open when the time is right.

And then she thinks of which servant she will have in the meantime, to chop her wood, and then, perhaps, she'll ask for another to do her laundry, because there's no doubt now Mr. Mole has plenty to look forward to.

Going back to her little house that morning, the field mouse, with all the things on her mind, takes a wrong turn through the passageways and comes upon the bird. It is an enormous thing and the field mouse is terrified, but then she sees it is fast asleep.

Creeping forward, ever so quietly the field mouse notices the stolen blanket, and the cross-stitches, sewn into its feathers.

Now she knows and understands that this is the girl's secret. Oh how she is filled with rage that little field mouse! It overpowers her. She has done so much for

that girl, from the moment she arrived on her
doorstep as an orphan, three months passed.

The field mouse visits the mole that night. Waking
him in his bed, she tells him that they are being
tricked and that there is a bird in a hidden passage,
and if he wants to keep his wife and have his way with
her again, then they must take the large candlestick
and carry it down the back stairs, along the passageway, to the bird.

Then, as the bird lies sleeping, they must ram the
candlestick, with its pointed end, straight through the
bird's heart.

And so it is done.

And the bird's eyes so very black, watch and glisten, in the torchlight.

Weeks pass and still the ground above is cold and the
sky wintry.

The field mouse looks out for changes in the girl.
But, it is the mole who changes.

Waking every night, his paws lash out, into the night
air. He can hear the screeching and the flapping. He is
sure the bird is in the corner, an enormous thing, and
the mole whimpers and calls out. Again and again.

But nothing is there and no-one comes. It is only the
sound of the girl singing during the day that stops
him shouting at the field mouse when she comes over.

And then the girl begins to disappear for great lengths
of time.

One night, the field mouse dreams of the house of the mole, looming up, dark and menacing. In her dream the shutters bang open and shut, the wind blows cold, and the swallows circle, round and round.

Bang, bang, bang! go those shutters.
Bang, bang, bang!

The field mouse wakes and gets up. She drinks from her little tap and her little claw, holding the little cup, is trembling. Then she paces and paces, from her little kitchen, into her little lounge and back again.

Back and forth, back and forth, until a path is born, in the threadbare carpet.

Over the weeks the girl watches them, the mole and the field mouse. She bides her time, waiting for the snow to melt. She waits, for she is very clever.

One morning, the field mouse walks the dark passageways to the house of the mole. She is exhausted, having had another bad night and walked the carpet bare.

Passing the place where the hidden passage lies she shivers a little. She is always relieved to get to the back stairs of the mole's and wander through the cook's kitchen.

The mole is having breakfast. He is cranky, his porridge dripping down his fur. He grunts when he sees the field mouse in the dim light.

'Has the girl already eaten her breakfast Mr. Mole?' asks the field mouse, timidly.

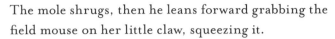

The mole shrugs, then he leans forward grabbing the field mouse on her little claw, squeezing it.

'She is no lady,' he hisses. 'She never comes when I call. Never!' He bares his sharp teeth at the field mouse. Then he lifts his old and musty newspaper up, so she cannot see him.

The field mouse nibbles on some toast, but she is not hungry. She longs for the girl to come. Just as she thinks to leave, she hears the girl's voice, singing from the stairs, of the great hall. The mole puts down his newspaper, and in a reverie, closes his eyes.

The singing moves nearer and then there is the girl, standing in the doorway. The girl is wearing a coat of feathers, carefully stitched and sewn. The field mouse realizes they are the feathers of the bird, from the hidden passageway.

The field mouse fills with a horror so deep that the room looms up all around.

The girl walks across the enormous room. Her singing stops when she gets to the shutters. She opens the shutters up, one by one.

Bang, bang, bang! go those shutters.

Then she opens up all the dirty windows.

Daylight pours in, filling up every darkened crevice of that enormous room. Sweet, perfumed air flows into all the mustiness and all the staleness, and the mole whimpers. His paws flaying out, in the air.

The girl turns towards the mole and the field mouse. Her coat of colours ignite in the rich daylight. Burnt orange, iridescent black and blue azure. How they shimmer, how they shine, in that new season light.

The field mouse cannot move.

The girl's eyes, very black, watch the field mouse and the mole, her keepers.

And in that moment the field mouse understands that the girl has known all along.

A slight breeze caresses the girl's hair, then her feathers, as she stands by the open window.

And the room looms up, a monstrous thing, round the little field mouse. And the mole whimpers more in his chair.

The field mouse finds herself calling out,
'It was us, it was us! Yes it was us!'

The girl, silent, listens to the field mouse and her confession. How she sobs that little field mouse, how she sobs.

When the field mouse stops weeping, the girl looks out of the window.

As the bird had lain dying, the girl had promised that she would make his feathers into a coat. 'You will ride upon my back Mr. Swallow,' she had sobbed. 'I will take you to the fields of green and the sweet, sweet corn, and the marshes and the bracken.'

The girl remembers how his eyes had glistened in the light!

'I will not leave you in this damp, rotten place, I promise.' And so her friend had died.

The girl is wearing a coat of feathers, carefully stitched and sewn.

Now, in her coat of feathers the girl looks out into the garden. The bulbs have burst: snowdrops, daffodils, crocuses and iris, their colors peeping out from the greenness of the grass.

'Winter is over,' she says. She stretches and flaps her coat. She turns back to the field mouse and the mole, her keepers no more. 'Can you hear them?'

The field mouse, terrified, sits frozen. Then, slowly she nods because she can hear the swallows, calling out beyond the green wood.

'They have come back,' the girl says. 'My family.' And she steps over the window ledge into the spring garden. Into the open world.

The field mouse scurries to the window and watches the girl walk out across the lawn and then onto the meadow. The girl disappears into the green wood.

The field mouse thinks of the dark passageways and all the things that have been carried, between her little house and the big, big house.

Then she thinks on her little doors and windows, opening up into the sweet, sweet air and into the spring fields above. And she wonders why it wasn't enough, more than enough, for a little field mouse.

*T*alk of the town

ews of the child had reached the King. She had been taken, under guard, to a convent far north and locked up in a tower.

The mother, mad with grief, the father broken.

Yet the King, pleased, gives all his soldiers two days off. A deep satisfaction settles over him. The problem has been dealt with, and swiftly at that.

Every morning, the King goes to his dressing chamber. An outfit, from the collection, waiting there. Each one carefully draped on a golden hanger, with a label attached, explaining the origin of the cloth and influence of the design.

The King's favourite is the Kashmir silk. A layered garment, woven in swirling patterns.

When he's walking, the King can hear the *swish, swish, swish.*

'I just love it,' he says to his dresser one particular morning. 'This is, indeed, my favourite.' He twirls around, towards the mirror, so he can admire his reflection in the glass.

'Your Majesty, the colour matches your eyes and the cut of the garment is so flattering,' his dresser murmurs.

'Do you think?' asks the King, twirling again.

When the dresser turns away, the King quickly leans forward, his head hitting the glass. He looks and looks, trying to discern his favourite fabric. It is to no avail.

He sees only his pallid skin, his paunch, and two swollen ankles.

'A wonderful day for a walk, Your Majesty.'

'Yes. Yes. Let us walk in the garden.
Let us have a picnic on the lawn.'

A servant is sent to the kitchen. The cooks to prepare an outdoor feast.

The King takes the path to the maze. He and his companions spend hours being lost and then found, much to their amusement.

It is hot. By mid afternoon the King feels faint. Lying down under the shade of a tree, he is served chilled water. Servants fan him. But the silk cloth that he cannot see seems to scratch at his skin.

The Egyptian cotton is sent for.

By the time it arrives, the King is ropable. Not waiting for the royal screen, the King flings off his garments. The servants scurry this way and that, after them.

Holding up his arms, the new outfit is carefully placed upon him.

'From the land of the Pharaohs,' his dresser reads from the label. 'You can feel the softness of the weave,' he adds.

But the cloth seems no different.
The King's skin is festering, red, raw.

The copper bath is sent for.

In it the King sits, in his Egyptian cotton outfit.
For the rest of the afternoon.

'Why am I so red?' he roars.

His chief advisor scurries forward.

'It is a hot day, Your Majesty. You have caught the sun. It is well that you sit in the bath, under the shade of the tree.'

'But I am red all over. It is as if I have been wearing nothing.'

'Your Majesty, the colour matches your eyes . . .'

Everyone freezes. Not a word is spoken.

'Well?'

'Perhaps the silk is not for outdoors, Your Majesty. Perhaps it is meant for indoors only.'

There is a murmur in the gathering, as if the thought has just occurred to all of them, and that it is a good one.

'The collection is in need of classification, Your Majesty. I suggest an added note to be written upon each label. Marked either 'indoor or outdoor.' This way, we can avoid the current unpleasantness.'

The King grunts. Closing his eyes, he can feel the water soothing against his skin. Despite his foul mood he drifts off to sleep.

The King starts dreaming. He can see himself asleep in his royal bed. Music is drifting through his window. The King, in his dream, watches himself waking, sitting up, turning to the sound. Then getting up and climbing out the royal window, in some strange daze.

The King watches himself, walking down the tower wall in his night shirt. His feet seemingly having some strange glue. And the music swirls around him. He can smell its sweetness, taste its sweetness. Like a honeyed spell.

Just as he is waking from the dream, the King remembers. The Procession from the fortnight before.

Despite all his efforts, it thunders down upon him, in his cooling, copper bath. The Moment.

And again. The Moment.
Despite his king-like effort, despite all his
king-like will, the Moment comes.

'He's wearing nothing, he's wearing nothing,' the
child had called out. Then, laughing and pointing
out her little finger, 'He's wearing nothing.'

The silence of the crowd.

'Why is he wearing nothing, Papa? Why? Why?'
The little girl was laughing and the King watched as
the guards carried her away, out of earshot.

The procession was cut short. The King returned to
the safety of his grounds. With all his advisors and
politicians apologising. For all their worth.

'A senseless, stupid child,' his chief advisor
informed him. 'How could one expect a child to
understand such craftsmanship?'

'She said I was wearing nothing.'

'A poor, uneducated little girl, Your Majesty.'

'Am I wearing nothing?'

'Do not think of it, Your Majesty! Think of the
envy of the crowd! You are the talk of the town!'

'Could have heard a pin drop,' his second advisor
piped in. 'A vision splendid, Your Majesty!'

'A vision splendid!' his court advisors echoed.

So the King, after the procession, had gone to bed,
wearing the Master Weaver's pyjamas. So light they
were on his skin that the King felt only the softness
of the sheet. And the touch of his wife, the Queen.
So silent she was. So shocked and silent.

The following morning, the King had ordered the child to be taken away, and so she was. To the convent, north in the country.

Far, far away.

'Your Majesty?'

'Mmmm?'

'Perhaps that is enough bathing for today? May I suggest supper with the Queen and an early night?'

The King, subdued, stands and is lifted from the bath. Waving the towels away, he walks back in his wet clothes. By the time he returns they are dry, but he insists on changing into a flounced-up number, from Venice.

He meets the Queen in the great hall.

Supper is served.

It is a quiet meal. The King can see his wife at the far end of the dining table, eating small mouthfuls.

'Don't you like the fish?' he calls out, his voice bouncing off the walls.

'The fish is fine.'

He can sense a certain tension.

'We had a lovely time in the garden, but I had too much sun. I ended up in the bath, under the tree.'

The King laughs.

The Queen puts her knife and fork down and slowly stands. Even from this distance the King is uneasy.

'Go and see the child,' she says. The force of her voice thunders through him. With that she leaves.

That night, the King sleeps alone. He is advised that the Queen is unwell and will perhaps see him in the morning but isn't promising anything.

Fast asleep, the dream from the afternoon returns. The King watches himself waking, climbing out the royal window, walking down the wall. The sweet honeyed music swirling round.

Far below, the King can see, the ground is moving.

Patter, patter, patter, patter. Another sound is near.

Patter, patter, patter, patter. How the music plays.

The King watches himself descend the wall on his glue-like feet, then lie face-down upon the earth. Hundreds of his servants and his soldiers dance on by.

Patter, patter, patter, patter. His bakers dance in threes.
Patter, patter, patter, patter. How the music plays.

Everyone is dancing over him, and around him, on their pattery little feet. Dancing to the Master Weaver's music.

The King wakes from his dream. The night is so still, as if it too is sleeping. Crawling to the window, the King leans out and farther out, looking far below.

Shadows and faint sounds greet him. The moon is dull. The King picks at his nightshirt, trying to feel the fabric of the cloth. He feels nothing but the heat from his burns.

He hears the voice of the Master Weaver in his head, haunting him.

The King spends the following day in bed. The Queen does not appear. He is informed that she is in her chambers and does not wish to be disturbed.

As the day passes the King feels dread creeping upon him. By nightfall, he is clammy. He requests a new nightshirt and that the bed sheets be changed. The window shutters are locked tight. The King, daring to hope a new day will put things right.

At dawn, the King finally falls asleep from sheer exhaustion. The same dream comes again and the King watches himself walk down the tower wall, with his two glued feet. The honeyed music is louder as the King lies down on the cold, dank, earth.

Patter, patter, patter, patter. His dressers dance on by.
Patter, patter, patter, patter. How the music plays.

Everyone is dancing over him, and around him, on their pattery little feet.

His politicians, his maids, his footmen and his guards are dancing in the cobbled streets and behind the market square. Dancing past the church and its steeple. Dancing past all the houses and all the animals in their mangers. Through the gate, beyond the wall, down the hill and over the rise. Way, way, way out of town. Dancing to the great mountain.

The King yearns to dance with them, on his two glued feet, under the dull moon.
Dance to the music that takes him to the great mountain. But the King, in his dream, can't move.

The King waking, is screaming, pulling at his nightshirt. The servants running in, helping him undress. Crouching in the corner, pulling at his neck, the King is calling out, 'Too tight, too tight!'

It is not until mid-morning that he is calm enough to believe that he is indeed completely and truly naked.

The King is carried to the dressing chamber. Breakfast has been cancelled.

'It is a fine day, Your Majesty, but not too hot. I have taken the liberty of classifying the garments. Will you spend your day indoors or outdoors?' the dresser asks.

'Indoors,' the King whispers.

'May I suggest the olive green, a light blend that will, should you wish, take a little of the outdoors if you change your mind.'

'That sounds fine,' croaks the King.

He is carefully dressed, by a number of dressers, as there is a certain listlessness about him.

'Look, Your Majesty. Another vision splendid.' His dressers clap a little, smiling and bowing.

The King gazes at his reflection. Two swollen ankles, his paunch and red skin greet him. The King is thinking of the dream and his servants' pattering feet.

He imagines them all, sitting in the darkness, with the door shut tight. With the Master Weaver's music playing round. Under the great mountain.

The King shuts his eyes. He is falling. Falling far below. Falling into the darkness, and the hardness, and all the effort, of his life.

'The green is a refreshing colour for this time of year, Your Majesty.'

The King lays his head upon the glass. 'It is a lovely green,' he says quietly. The King can feel the coolness of the glass against his head and it feels so sweet. Just that little bit of cool against his head.

The dressers in the dressing chamber cannot move. They are watching their King, running his head, from side to side, against the coolness of that glass. And they wonder about him. What is happening in his head.

'Do you have anything in wool?'

A dresser, shocked, bows. 'Of course, Your Majesty. The Master Weaver left a wonderful winter collection, but the weather . . .'

'I'm taking a trip. I'm going north. It will be cooler there. Pack the warmer outfits and place them in my carriage. I will be leaving after lunch.'

His wife has left a note on the downstairs table.

'Gone to my sister's. Not sure when I'll be back. Don't wait up for me.'

The King has a light lunch. The carriage is ready. In it he sits. 'To the convent,' he says to the driver. 'Make haste.'

News of the King's travelling quickly spreads through all the towns and villages. People line the streets, hoping for a glimpse of the vision splendid. All have been instructed to remain silent and bow their heads as the royal carriage passes. Most do, except for the small children, but their eyes and mouths are quickly covered by their mothers. Everyone knows what has happened to the child.

In his carriage, the King sits on the royal blanket, seemingly in his olive green outfit. That which can take both a little of the outdoor and a little of the indoor, so great is its versatility.

From time to time the King waves his royal wave at the passers-by. He has never felt so completely and utterly alone. The further north he travels the darker and more strange his mood becomes. He begins picking at his skin, murmuring to himself, 'a lovely green, a lovely green.'

By the time he reaches the mountain the King is blue with cold. He orders the carriage forward, on the high road. He can see the convent, way on high, and beyond the snow-capped peaks.

The royal carriage ascends.

'Open the gates. Open the gates. The King is here, the King is here!'

The convent gates open and the carriage enters the courtyard. The King is helped from his carriage. So cold he is, from the mountain air, he can barely move. More garments from the collection are flung on him as he makes his way to a small grate in the door. But of course they make no difference.

His footmen bang on the door.

'The King is here. The King is here!'

The grate is opened and a nun appears.

Well, this nun has neither seen a man nor a naked one at that. She screams so loudly that all the birds in the courtyard take flight.

'The King is here to see the child! Open the door!'

The door is opened and the King, blue with cold, steps over the nun, who has just fainted.

Well, those nuns in that convent have never had a day like this one. A naked man, a King at that, walking through the great hall, then the banquet chamber, through the kitchens and along the cloisters, looking for the child. Everywhere he walks the nuns are screaming and running this way and that, trying to keep away from such a sight.

The King, by this time is delirious, muttering 'the child, the child,' until a nun, who has seen a little

Together they sit, the child and the King. Upon that little bed.

of the outside world, takes him and leads him up a spiral staircase, to a room at the top of the tower.

In it the child sits. Upon her bed. When the King enters, with his footmen and his guards the little girl is frightened. But she does not move.

The King sends his guards away. 'I am very cold,' whispers the King.

Despite her fear, the little girl gets up and leads him to her bed. He sits and she wraps some blanket around him.'Thank you,' he whispers.' The King is so very grateful to her.

She wraps a little more blanket around him, and then a little more. Then, being brave, holds his hand. 'Where are your clothes?' she asks in a small voice.

The King can only shake his head and weep a little. He takes off his crown.

The child gets up and walks to the door and opens it. There is a kind and sensible nun waiting there. She hands the little girl a freshly laundered nun's habit, about the King's size. She takes it to him.

'There is this,' she says. She offers it to him.

With her help, the King dresses in the habit. The frock, the cotton undergarments, the veil.

'It will keep your head warm,' whispers the little girl. The King sobs. She gently places his crown on top of his head again. Together they sit, the child and the King. Upon that little bed. In the tower room on the mountain top.

She keeps him company. Whilst he waits. For all his king-like senses, to return.

The Red Shoes

And those shoes, with the little feet in them, danced
over the fields and into the deep forest.[1]

They danced along the path and then *splash, splash, splash* into the little brook.

And there, they danced and they got heavier with all the water and so they rested, amongst the fishes and the water-grass, very, very quietly.

The fish, in the brook, nibbled at the feet, until there was only bone.

The following week, a young boy comes with a fishing rod and catches one enormous, shiny fish and then one red shoe. The shoe jumps about in his bucket, like the fish, so he puts a stone upon them both and carries the bucket home to his mother.

'That is a fine, fat fish you have caught, my son. Enough for us to feast on for at least two suppers.' His mother takes the fish out, laying it on the table.

Then the shoe jumps out and she's chasing it around the room until she has it cornered. She throws a blanket over it and puts a chair upon it and then she sits upon the chair, all breathless.

The boy tells her about catching the red shoe in the

1. from *The Red Shoes*, by Hans Christian Andersen.

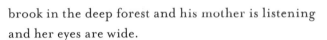

brook in the deep forest and his mother is listening and her eyes are wide.

Bending over and lifting up the corner of the blanket, she can see the shoe, quivering, and she's quickly dropping the blanket down.

'There's a powerful magic in that shoe, Son, and with one shoe caught, then perhaps there is another. There might be some use for us in finding it.'

The woman carefully locks the door on the way out and she and her son set off. They go back to the brook, in the deep green forest, and there they sit and fish. They catch three more large and shiny fish but not another shoe.

'No matter,' the woman says. 'We have four fine fish and one magic shoe, and we will have a feast and celebrate.'

That night, the woman invites the villagers to her table. She has roasted the four fine fish in wild dill and rosemary and in the middle of her table she has placed a cloche and in it she has put, with great difficulty, the red shoe.

How it jumps about under the heavy glass and it *tap, tap, taps* upon it, and the woman, being a wise woman, speaks to it and says, 'I will go fishing again tomorrow and for three days after and I will bring you back your other half, but play a little tune for me now, upon the glass, one that we all can dance to.'

And so the villagers come to her table and they feast on the fish and the red shoe taps a merry beat upon the glass and one old neighbour takes out his fiddle and another neighbour her whistle and how they dance, those villagers, until three o'clock in the morning. Dragging their weary feet back to their houses and falling upon their beds, snoring their heads off.

And the cows moo in the barn and the hens are unfed and the dogs without water until the villagers are able to rise again, mid-afternoon, and go back to their chores.

After the festivities, the woman places a blanket upon the cloche, and the shoe goes quiet, like a little bird in a cage.

But when she takes the blanket off, the shoe jumps about, so she says, 'Play a pretty beat, and I will sing a song for with all the chores I'm doing I could do with some fine music.'

So the shoe plays a pretty beat upon the glass and the woman's singing her songs and there's a spring in her step, that's for sure. Even though her neighbours are still all sleeping.

In the afternoon, she and her son go back into the deep forest, back to the brook. There they sit and wait for the fish to nibble, and they talk about the fine party and that if they catch four more fish they'll have another for it has been many a year since such dancing in their little village.

This time, they catch five fat fish, but no shoe, and the woman says, 'No matter, we will have another party and dance till four in the morning at least.'

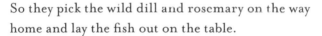

So they pick the wild dill and rosemary on the way home and lay the fish out on the table.

That evening, the villagers come again, bringing more things to add to the feast and the one red shoe, in the cloche, *tap, tap, tap*s upon the glass, and the villagers are dancing and singing and they can feel the goodness of the dancing and the singing and it's all getting into their bones and that is a very fine thing because doing chores all the time can be wearying.

Then they all go home, falling upon the bed and the cows and the dogs and the hens and the geese and the ducks have to wait again until evening this time.

The following afternoon, when the mother and son go down to the brook in the deep, green forest there is a man, standing there, in the glade.

. . . and they can feel the goodness of the dancing and the singing and it's all getting into their bones . . .

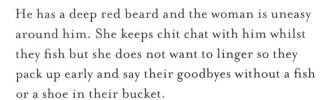

He has a deep red beard and the woman is uneasy around him. She keeps chit chat with him whilst they fish but she does not want to linger so they pack up early and say their goodbyes without a fish or a shoe in their bucket.

Back in the kitchen, she lifts up the blanket and she tells the shoe that it might be a little longer than she hoped, her finding its mate, and that she will wait three days until she goes back.

The shoe is very quiet when she is speaking to it and she, knowing it is a magic shoe, respects it and talks to it as if it is another person in the room. And so she waits.

On the fourth day, she and her son go back to the brook. There is no sign of the man.

They fish for five hours and catch five fat fish, and even though the shoe is not caught the woman feels it is just biding its time and will soon be found, that's for sure.

When she goes back she lays the fish upon the table and chops the wild, wild herbs but there is a feeling about her, this day, so the woman uncovers the blanket and tells the shoe why she waited three days.

She tells the shoe of the man in the glade and his red, red beard, and how she felt uneasy. The shoe jumps about so, hitting the glass hard, so hard, she's thinking it will break.

And the woman knows something has happened, because the shoe is quivering and shaking so. She's singing a gentle song, and opening up the

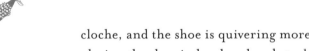

cloche, and the shoe is quivering more and she's placing the shoe in her hand and stroking it and then she sees, the little bones all scattered inside it.

A terrible dread, so deep, comes up inside her.

Singing a little more, she takes the little bones out from the shoe and places them upon the table, next to all the big, fat fish and the wild dill and rosemary.

Then she places the shoe back in the cloche and covers it with the blanket.

She pieces all of those little bones together because not only is this woman wise, she is also very clever.

There laid out on the large wooden table are the bones of a foot. It is a beautiful and delicate thing, and the woman is knowing something very bad has happened.

That night, she goes alone, into the deep dark wood, with only the moonlight to guide her. She takes a fishing rod and sits by the brook and she fishes for the other shoe, fishes and fishes, and just before dawn, just as light is about to break, she catches it.

It's jumping about so in her bucket and she places a rock upon it and sings to it, knowing what a terrible thing there is inside, and just before the edge of the wood she sees the man, with the red beard, staring out from above his fire.

She is uneasy and her power is surging through her because she does not like this man at all.

He smiles at her from the distance and stands and walks to her and she notices the shoe, in her bucket, has gone very, very quiet.

. . . just before the edge of the wood she sees the man, with the red beard, staring out . . .

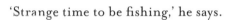

'Strange time to be fishing,' he says.

'Strange time to be watching,' says she.

He steps closer and tries to look in her bucket,
but she turns a little away so he can't see.

'What did you catch?'

'Some supper,' she says, and moves to be on her way.

He catches her arm and holds it, tightly. 'Fancy
sharing some?' he says, and he looks at her behind
that beard and licks his lips a little. She can feel his
power in his fingers, pressing into her.

Then she says something very surprising.

'Come for supper tonight. We are having a fine feast.
With music and dancing,' and she curtsies a little.

For there is some knowing in her, this fine and
clever woman, some knowing of a very dark kind,
and she's trusting her instincts in this moment, to
guide her.

He bows and steps back a little and says, 'Dancing?
That's the devil's work, but I will come and feast,
that's for sure.'

They leave each other, just at the edge of the wood.

Later that day, she watches the red shoes in the
cloche. So happy they are to be together again,
spinning around, moving this way and that way, in
perfect harmony.

The woman has never seen anything so elegant and
refined. She sings to them gentle songs from her
childhood and they both are quiet, and she lifts the
cloche and takes the other red shoe out and sure

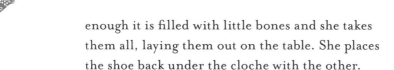

enough it is filled with little bones and she takes them all, laying them out on the table. She places the shoe back under the cloche with the other.

Putting all the bones where they need to be, and sure enough two little feet lay, upon the table, with the fish and the herbs and she wonders what has happened to the rest of the little person they belonged to.

Her son comes in, carrying the bucket from feeding the hens and his mother wipes her hands on the apron and the boy stands in the door way and the light is there behind him, and he says, 'Mother, Mother, who is singing?'

'No-one is singing,' she says.

But the boy is shaking his head and he goes to the table and puts his ear right near the bones and says, 'Mother, Mother, the bones are singing, the bones are singing.'

And the bones sing to the little boy their story.
And the boy tells the story to his mother.
They sing of the man who overpowered them
and they sing of the other who cut them.

His mother asks the boy, 'What does this man look like, the one who overpowered them?', and they sing back to the son, 'A man, with a red, red beard.'

She's sitting upon the stool, that wise and clever woman. For it is indeed a terrible tale that has been told.

And the woman thinks on the little girl that the feet belonged to and she thinks on the man whom she begged to cut them free and then she thinks on the man who overpowered her in the beginning and she's thinking that it is a terrible, terrible tale but as luck would have it, she's caught one of the fish in this story and she's not going to let him get away.

She tells the shoes what she wants to do and they agree to it by skipping round and round.

She asks her neighbour to come and help because there's not only a feast to prepare, there's a trap to be laid, and still the dog needs his water and the hens need feeding and there will be dancing in the streets, she's thinking, for three days at least, after all this.

She grinds the bones into a fine powder and fixes it in a drink. She goes and tells the man to come early.

She roasts the fish and prepares the table. She puts the cloche, under the blanket, under the chair, in the corner.

The man comes early.

She sits him at the table and says to him, 'You're a man who likes to travel and walk the long and lonely road. Here is a fine drink prepared for you, for indeed you must be thirsty.'

The man drinks the drink and some is dribbling down his beard and his eyes are dark and lonely.

The woman takes out the cloche with the red shoes in it, placing it upon the table. She takes the cover off.

The shoes are still.

The man is staring at the shoes, and there is an evil grin upon his face, and he says, 'I see you, Woman, there is surely the devil inside,' and he raises his hands and she knows he has a power in them and she's hoping the shoes are going to do what they do, for now the bones are inside him.

How could she have doubted them, those red, red shoes. For they have waited long, so long, for this moment.

They start to hop and skip and jump about in the glass cloche and the man's feet start twitching and jumping about and sure enough his feet and legs are following the movement of the red shoes and he's up and dancing about and shouting and knocking things off the table and the woman cries:

'Son, Son, get the door, get the door,' and the son opens the door wide and the man dances out and then back in again and the red shoes in the cloche are now running around in it so fast and the woman looks out the window, for the man is back outside again and the man is running into the pigsty and falling over, covered in muck.

Then his feet are dragging him back out again and then running around the graveyard and then into the little church, and the shoes in the cloche are so excited the woman thinks *oh, let's have them out for a little while*, so she takes the cloche off and they run amok in her kitchen and her bedroom and then out into the streets they go, and the woman is thinking of the man with the red, red beard and where he is with all the running.

The villagers come and feast on the fish and

everyone dances for four days, and it is quite a thing to put the red shoes back in the cloche but the woman manages it.

And the villagers have a spring in their step forever more, because there are plenty more of the those fish to feast on and dances to be had, and from time to time the woman puts the blanket over the cloche so the red shoes can rest, but not for too long, for they are so very happy to be dancing.

Oh, indeed, they love to dance!

The villagers have dancing most nights and it is so good for their bones and the dogs and the hens and the cows and the sheep, and the geese have had to learn to become, very, very patient.

Then his feet are dragging him back out again . . .

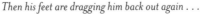

Duck Boy

Han got up early to milk the goat. It was a perfect summer's day and the lake was calling him.

His mother made him a picnic. His two sisters would follow, after their chores.

Han gathered his fishing rod and bucket. He shut the gate behind him so the dog wouldn't follow. He waddled along the dusty road down to the lake. Han could see the lake waters sparkling between the tall rushes. He loved being near the water.

The lake was his favourite place.

He sat down on the sand and opened his little box full of worms. He quickly looked around. No one else was there yet. He put a nice juicy worm in his mouth and another on his fish hook.

'Quack, quack,' he said very quietly.
'Quack, quack, quack.'

He buried his duck feet into the sand. He dropped his line into the clear still water. Geese flew across the blue sky and he watched them flying. Han tried to imagine how it would be to fly so high like that.

Looking down on the lake and the road, looking down on the house he lived in with his family, looking down on his village in the valley in the mountains.

Han opened up the box of worms again and picked himself another. He could hear the other children coming along the road, shouting and yelling. He quickly ate the worm, clamping the lid of the box tight and putting it back in his pocket.

He swallowed the quack that was rising in his throat, swallowed it right down and deep.

'Han! Han!' The village children ran by him, some jumping into the water, others plopping down around him. Laughing and chatting.

Han smiled and nodded and said hello to his next-door neighbour William, and little Clara who lived just down the road.

'Been swimming yet Han?' William asked. Han shook his head. 'Not yet.'

'Nothing's in your bucket,' said Clara, frowning as she sat down next to him.

His legs and her legs golden brown. Side by side. Her feet, with her ten little perfect toes, buried in the sand. Next to his.

'I like you,' she whispered and Han squirmed, like one of the worms in his box.

He wanted to bury himself deep in the sand. He hoped she'd go swimming soon.

The rod was tugging a little and he picked it up and

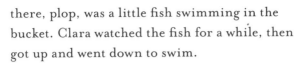

there, plop, was a little fish swimming in the
bucket. Clara watched the fish for a while, then
got up and went down to swim.

All morning Han fished.

At noon, he went for a paddle in the shallows,
not too deep. Then he ate his picnic. His two sisters
were down there now, talking with their friends
and laughing, lying about in the sun.

Han wandered along the lake shore, picking up bits
of shell from the edge and looking at them. Three
of the other village children followed him and did
the same.

At four o'clock, a new boy appeared at the lake.
He was the cousin of Han's neighbour. He came
from a large town three days' journey away from
the village. Han saw that the new boy was tall and
strong, maybe five years older than him.

He heard someone call out 'Peter.'

Han watched Peter talking with the others and
swimming in the lake where the water was deep.
He watched him diving from the rocks and
swimming underneath the water, far longer than
anyone else.

He watched him swim to the shore, waddling
proudly out and shaking himself dry.

That night, Han said good night to his mother and
father and went upstairs to his bedroom.

He opened up the window on the still summer
night and the moon shone down. He listened to the

sounds of the village all around him and the cows mooing in the meadow.

Han gathered the sheets on his bed and made himself a little nest under the window. Just before he fell asleep he thought about the boy, Peter, from the big town.

'Quack, quack,' he whispered sleepily, 'quack, quack.'

The following morning, after milking the goat, Han again went down to the lake. No one was there, and he ate three juicy worms and quacked a little more than usual before the others came along.

Peter arrived with William and glanced at Han fishing.

'Have you got any worms?' Peter asked. Han nodded and showed him his little box full.

Peter took one and popped it in his mouth. 'Thanks,' he said.

It was hot, too hot for fishing. Han wandered down to the water's edge and paddled a little in the shallows. He could see Peter jumping off the rocks and diving down again, into the deepest part of the lake. Diving down. Way, way down.

That night, in his nest under the window, Han thought of Peter. The way he'd taken the worm and eaten it, and the way he dived, his duck feet glistening as he launched himself from the rocks.

Han sat up and looked at all the shoes his father had made him, year after year, carefully shaped and crafted.

That night, in his nest under the window, Han thought of Peter.

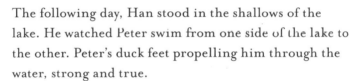

The following day, Han stood in the shallows of the lake. He watched Peter swim from one side of the lake to the other. Peter's duck feet propelling him through the water, strong and true.

That night Han flew from his open window into the full moon. He flew so high and bright.

And he looked down on his little village and the mountains and the towns as he flew higher and higher. And the geese came to keep him company and the mountain eagle and flocks of white swans.

They were gathered all around Han, flying high and away, into the shiny, silvery moon.

When Han woke the following morning, his arms felt stiff and sore. He didn't know if he had dreamt a dream or if he had truly flown from his window into the full moon.

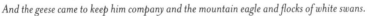

And the geese came to keep him company and the mountain eagle and flocks of white swans.

His arms were so tired he had difficulty milking the goat. He quacked and ruffled his clothes, grumpily.

Han's mother asked him to pick up some meat from the butcher's before he went down to the lake. He put on some shoes and walked along the street into the market square.

Peter was there lying on a bench. He had a hat perched on his head and was chewing a grass reed.

People walked past him and Peter had not a care in the world, lying along the wooden bench with his two webbed feet, jutting over the edge, crossed over.

Han watched Peter from across the market square. He watched him as he lay there in the sun. Han looked down at his own feet in his father's carefully crafted shoes.

He went to the butcher's shop and bought the meat.

Down at the lake, Han ate the whole box of worms himself. Then he stood and walked to the lake's edge.

He allowed himself to quack as much as he wanted as he walked, further and further out, deeper and deeper into the lake until his webbed feet struck out, into the void. Han could feel the power of his feet underneath him, pulling the water, and he swam further and further out.

Then, taking a deep breath, he dived down into the depths amongst the lake grasses.

How long he stayed there! He swam with the amber fish. He plucked at the sand looking for treasure.

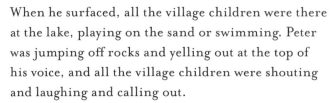

When he surfaced, all the village children were there at the lake, playing on the sand or swimming. Peter was jumping off rocks and yelling out at the top of his voice, and all the village children were shouting and laughing and calling out.

Little Clara was standing by the shore watching. Han waved from the deep and he could feel the strength in his feet as he raised his arm to her.

The water moved over him and around him and cooled his olive skin. He felt strong and alive.

'Quack, quack,' Han called at the top of his voice. 'Quack, quack, quack!'

Then, taking a deep breath, he dived down into the depths amongst the lake grasses.

White, White World

ow long have you been dead?'

'Just,' she says.

The boy, turning, is looking out the window.
The huddled figure below is unmoving.
Like a headless snowman, he's thinking.

Turning back, he's looking at the girl. Her eyes are
bright, hollow. There is a creeping pink of colour
in her cheeks. Her skin is white, white, white.

'I've been watching you,' he says. 'These past three
days. I've been watching you try and sell your
little matches.'

'I know.' And the words send a shiver through him.

Climbing up to the window ledge she sits beside him.

'Would you like some of my blanket?'

She nods, quickly taking the corner that he's offering
and wrapping it around her boney shoulders.
She is shivering.

'Come closer,' he says, and is surprised by his boldness.
She nestles into him, laying her cheek against his
chest. He can feel his heart thumping.

Her hair is soft and its curls fall against him, hanging over his arms. He likes her being there. She does not ask anything of him. For the first time, in a long time, he feels relieved.

Together the two children look out through the thick glass into the white, white world. The snow falls thickly, heaping in drifts, against the lamp posts below.

'Look, they're digging for me,' she says.

The children look down, watching as people gather round the headless snowman. A man is using a spade and calling out. The people, silent, are shivering in their furs.

'You've been looking down at me and I've been looking up at you.' She's giggling. 'I've been looking at your big house and the tree in your hall and I have seen the golden goose you had for dinner.'

'Look, they're digging for me,' she says.

'I didn't have much,' he says.

She sits up, looking at him. Then she plants a sweet little kiss, right on his blue lips. 'I had such a lovely dream after. Even though I was so cold.' She tells him of her dream of the dinner goose. Walking round with knives and forks. Sticking in him, all over. Honking, honking.

Now the boy is giggling too.

When the story is done they lay quiet together again.

'Will you stay a while?'

'I'm not sure,' she says, 'but if I do, I'd like a bath.'

He nods because even though she's perfect there's a musty smell about her. He knows she'd like the soap that smells of apples.

'I'll get the servant to bring the bath up, in the morning.' He's feeling relieved all over again and it's a blessing. It's her presence that calms him, and everything about her calls him to her. As if, finally and at last, he has found his home.

When the young boy wakes he sees his mother by his bedside. She is gently wiping his brow with her lace handkerchief. He feels the dread seeping through him. His words are now coming out. Breathless. Strained. 'Bath. Water. Apple soap.'

His mother looks to her mother and it's that look he's grown used to over the past few months. Where a thousand words are spoken, only silent.

'Bath, water, apple soap.'

'Shhh, shhh, my darling boy. Oh I cannot bear it, I cannot bear it!' his mother cries.

She is weeping again and the boy feels himself drowning in her waterfall of sorrow. He is gasping for breath.

'Get the doctor, get the doctor,' his mother cries again, and the servant runs out to get the doctor.

The doctor listens to the young boy's heart and checks his pulse. Looking into his eyes, he says quietly. 'No change. Perhaps a little worse.'

And the doctor's head bends over and it takes all the young boy's efforts to pat his head of grey, whispering, 'It's alright, it's alright.'

Then the boy wakes again and his grandmother is standing in the room. Beside her is the copper bath, full of water. She is looking at him and her eyes are shining. She says, 'I don't know what is happening but when I got here this morning I ordered the servant to bring up the bath. I couldn't find the apple soap. But I have the blossom.'

The young boy smiles at his kind and loving grandmother. Then she leaves. He watches the fire for a while. It's dancing round the room, warm and cosy. He feels so happy. There's a splashing in the corner and he's knowing it is she, returning. *Drip, drip, drip.*

He won't look, until he hears her voice.
Drip, drip, drip. Splash, splash.

'Come on. The bubbles smell of blossom.
We can tell each other stories whilst we bathe.'

Getting up from his sick bed, this little boy is walking across the room on his little stick legs.

Taking off his nightdress, he is naked. She's watching him come and she's whispering,

'You are almost as skinny as me, but not quite — and you are beautiful.'

Hopping into one end of the bath, she is in the other. Little matchsticks float round the boy and girl.

'Sorry,' she says. 'I forgot they were in my pockets.'

Then he's seeing her, wearing her rags.

'Turn round,' he says.

Turning around, her hair in ringlets, hanging down her back. His hands are trembling. It's not easy. One by one, undoing the buttons on her blouse. 'Lift up your arms.' It takes all his strength. Pulling that blouse off. Her skin underneath.
Grey and glistening.

And she stands and he closes his eyes. When he opens them her rags of skirt have dropped all around them on the floor, in tatters.

Sitting in the blossom bath, they tell each other stories. She tells him of her parents and of her many sisters and brothers. He is sad a little, for he is an only child.

He tells her of his father who is a rich merchant, and his mother and grandmother and about his dog that he had when he was tiny.

Then they talk of the town in which they live and the streets that they know and the ones that they don't and the shopkeepers and the markets and the church-es and the gardens, and they talk of all the things they love and find interesting until they can talk no more.

Then she sings him songs and he blows bubbles in

the air and their little bodies float in the water full of matches. They laugh and play silly games until the water gets too cold.

Climbing out, they look at one another in their nakedness. Marvelling at the wondrous things that they are. With their skinny little legs and arms and their flat chests and the bits between their legs that are different. Then she kisses him again on his pale blue lips and he feels like he is floating round the room and bouncing off the corners, like a little cloud.

On their little stick legs, they wander back to the window, sitting on the ledge, wrapping themselves in blankets.

'I've gone,' she says looking down on the lamp post outside, to where she was once before. 'I'm all gone.'

'I wonder who took you away?'

And she starts to shimmer like a star and he watches on with wondrous eyes, calling out, 'Are you going now too?', and she calls back, all shimmering, 'I'm not sure.'

When the young boy wakes it is evening. There's a storm raging on the other side of the thick glass. He knows he is being carried, and he wonders if it's to his coffin and he hopes it smells sweet, he'd like it to be sweet, like the sugar on a pancake.

Lying back in his bed, he can hear the waterfall of sorrow and it is thundering down all over him and yet he does not drown this time. It washes over him and through him and he feels how loved he is in this strange, strange land.

'Grandmother?'

'Yes my darling.'

'Tell me a story.'

His grandmother tells him of an orchard that she once knew as a child, a cherry orchard, and each year she would go with her mother and father and sisters and they would pick cherries and fill their baskets and lie on blankets afterwards.

Other families would come and do the same, and after they had eaten everyone would dance and sing and play music and they would form big, wide circles, around the cherry trees and dance around them as if they too were people. And his grandmother, as a little girl, called them cherry people, and she would wander off, a little way, but not too far and wrap her

His grandmother tells him of an orchard that she once knew as a child.

little arms around their trunks. And she'd whisper stories to them and her secrets, until her mother called her. And the young boy hears every word his grandmother is speaking, and each word is soaking into his skin.

He hears a man's voice and knows it is his father and he wonders about him, who he truly was, because to him he is just a passer-by, but with a name.

'Father,' he says. He can feel a breath on him. 'Father,' he says again. And he likes saying it, knowing that he can say that name and that it means somebody is here, breathing on him.

'Mother, Mother.' And he feels how he likes saying that word too, but he knows his mother inside out so it is different. His grandmother is singing and she is there, the match girl, standing right behind his singing grandmother. She is smiling and waving and glimmering like a star, and he gets up from his bed and dances to her, on his two match legs.

'Not yet, not yet,' she's laughing, and she takes his little hand, leading him back to his big bed. Tucking him back in, eyes twinkling, she's whispering in his ear. 'I'm hungry.'

When he wakes again the room is empty. Except for her. Sitting by the fire on a little chair. She is wearing rags and they are clean, smelling sweet.

'Come. Eat. There is such a feast before us.'

He gets out of bed for he is ravenous. The room smells of golden goose, and upon the little table piled, potatoes, in their jackets. Thick gravy, cream and cherry pie and roast beef.

. . . and he is leaning into her this time, with his little head upon her chest.

She tucks in and he tucks in. Each mouthful is divine and they can't talk to one another because their mouths are so full. Their eyes are shining. Everything feels so good. He eats and eats until he can eat no more.

She lies back on the chair and pats her round, round belly. Burping, he giggles and burps too. Then they laugh and get up, wrapping their arms around one another. Dancing around the room.

He tells her all his secrets and she tells him all her stories. Their little heads are touching and they breathe each other in. They have never felt so completely known, until this moment. Climbing onto the window sill again, the two children are looking out into the white, white world.

She is wrapping the blanket around him this time, and he is leaning into her this time, with his little head upon her chest. But he hears no beating heart. He, looking into her eyes that say everything, understands all that is spoken, only silent.

'The man came, with the horse and the cart,' she's saying. 'He was the one who took me away.'

'Will he take me away too?' he asks.

She shakes her head, quickly. 'No. No. You will have a dozen black horses and a carriage made of glass and a hundred red, red roses placed upon you.'

And the two children gaze out together at the world beyond, both full of wonder at the thought of it.

Song
of the Nightingale

In the forest of the tall trees, the Emperor waits.

The blackened night without a star waits with him.
The shadowed moon way up above waits with him too.
In the forest, far away, a bird calls out.

But it is not the nightingale.

The Emperor remembers the morning just passed.
He remembers waking up in his death chamber and
speaking to the servant.'Good morning,' he'd said.

The servant looked around, confused. 'Good morning,'
he had said again, smiling encouragingly. The servant
had run screaming from the room.

In that moment, the Emperor had known
it was going to be quite a day.

He remembers now raising himself up from his death bed,
no longer a corpse but a living man. It had felt wondrous.
The sweetness of breath. The glorious feeling of just being
alive! He had opened up the shuttered windows and let the
sunlight in. Bathed in golden light, anointed.

And then he had stood there. It had all come about because
of the nightingale. The nightingale! Oh, how its song had
reached for him in those strange and haunted death lands.

Oh, how it had reached! Carrying him back on its bird call song. Carrying him back, renewed. *Whoo, whoo. Whoo, whoo.*

An owl calls out in the tall treed forest. Not far from where the Emperor waits. *Whoo, whoo. Whoo, whoo.*

The Emperor shivers a little from the eerie sound. Where, oh where, is the nightingale? His mind drifts back to the morning. He had left his death chamber and walked along the palace corridor. Doormen had fainted, one after the other, as he'd walked by. His dogs had appeared and run excitedly to him, almost knocking him over.

'There, there Manchu, down Gang Gang, down, my sweet Minze.' He had laughed, wrangling and scampering with them, jumping all around their wagging tails. He'd decided to take them out, into the palace gardens and play with them some more.

Outside it had been glorious and the Emperor, with his dogs following, had skipped all around the garden beds. 'I am alive! I am alive!' he'd shouted out, beating his chest.

All of the palace windows had opened. A hundred faces looked down at him, all in disbelief.

'I am alive! I am alive!' he'd shouted out to them all. The Prime Minister's face had been particularly pale. The Emperor had thought, *not yet my friend, not yet.* For the Emperor knew his Prime Minister very, very well.

'It is I, your Emperor!' he had shouted out. 'Back from the dead, the dead!'

And all the faces became paler still, except for a small boy, who waved to him.

The Empress, his wife, was nowhere to be seen which was not unusual. They had lived separate lives these past few years. But the Emperor was bursting with joy so he'd skipped to her quarters, shouting, 'Dear one, dear one, it is I, arisen from my death bed, it is I!'

He'd opened up the double doors and walked into the Empress's chambers. There she had lain. Upon her bed. Her chamber maids weeping and the doctor standing useless in the corner. The Empress had been gripped by a fever, so deep that the Emperor had known instantly. She was in the death lands, the place that he had just come from, and the nightingale had not sung to her, to bring her back.

He startles now when he hears a mournful cry from somewhere deep in the forest. There! There! A sound. A call? A song?

The Emperor stands, ready to follow this time. But it is a cry of some strange beast, tormented. The Emperor thinks back to his wife. Brushing the astonished Doctor's questions aside he'd insisted, 'I am well, I am

Oh, how its song had reached for him in those strange and haunted death lands.

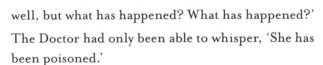

well, but what has happened? What has happened?'

The Doctor had only been able to whisper, 'She has been poisoned.'

For the Emperor sees now that plots had been crafted, schemes had been made and words had been whispered as he had lain dying, on his death bed.

And so a poisoned chalice had been carefully placed on the Empress's bedside table. In the middle of the night, his wife had drunk it, thinking it was water. Now, sitting in the dark, the Emperor wonders why he has grown so cold with his wife, these past few years. Why he has turned away, for she does love him so.

'Wait for me,' the Emperor whispers into the darkness. 'Wait for me my love. I will bring you back the nightingale and its song. Just wait for me and hold on.'

There is a distant honk as geese fly high overhead. Where is the nightingale? The Emperor feels the strangeness of the coarsely woven shirt he is wearing.

'You must change into other clothes,' the maid of the kitchen had whispered. 'There are many who believe you to be dead and everything has been arranged because of it.' She had pushed the shirt urgently into the Emperor's hands when she had returned to the storeroom. He'd been hiding there all afternoon.

'Go now, go,' the doctor had whispered. 'I will keep watch over the Empress, but go, hide!' They had run like thieves, he and the maid, through the kitchens of crackling goose, out past the pigsties and the kitchen gardens and then beyond the wall, into the forest of the tall trees.

'Quickly, quickly,' the maid of the kitchen had whispered and she'd hidden behind a boulder.

The Emperor followed just as horsemen had appeared over the rise. The horses had walked past and the Emperor heard one of the men say, 'Well he is dead — is he not? — and the new Emperor will soon be crowned.'

Then they had all laughed and talked about him, the Emperor as if he were already dead. There'd been contempt in their voices as they thought him a vain and self-serving man who lived in a porcelain castle and had a tendency to flog those around him when he did not get his way. The kitchen maid had been watching him as he'd listened to the men and the Emperor had wondered if she'd thought these things as well.

'Now we must hurry again,' she'd whispered as the men on horseback had passed by and they'd run through the ever darkening wood until there was a salt smell in the air. 'Wait here, for hereabouts the nightingale will sing,' she'd said. 'Wait here.'

She had left him, hours ago now, sitting on a rock, wearing the coarsely woven shirt, stolen from a stable hand's cupboard. There! There! Now! So faint, so faint, yet so pure. A single note cuts between the empty spaces of the trees. The Emperor stands, his heart pounding for he knows it is the nightingale! The nightingale!

Though there is darkness all around, he closes his eyes. There it is, the trill, the trill, and then the warble and then another single note and the Emperor, despite his anguish, clasps his hands as he listens to this night time symphony. He runs and stumbles in the blackness, and gets up and runs again. As quickly as he can.

'My friend, my friend, it is I, your Emperor, all lost in this dark and lonely forest,' he calls out.

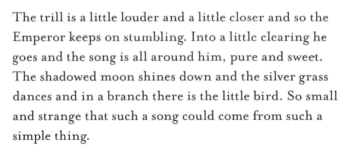

The trill is a little louder and a little closer and so the Emperor keeps on stumbling. Into a little clearing he goes and the song is all around him, pure and sweet. The shadowed moon shines down and the silver grass dances and in a branch there is the little bird. So small and strange that such a song could come from such a simple thing.

'My friend, my friend.' The Emperor kneels down in the shadowed silver light and bows his head. And he prays to that little grey bird and tells his story of plots, and schemes and his poisoned wife, and the palest of faces the prime minister. He begs the nightingale to return to the castle with him, and sing its song. The little bird flies around him and pushes at him with its wings and it sings a little note, a simple note for him to follow.

As he stumbles along the paths, following the sound of the nightingale just ahead, the Emperor thinks again on his wife and his coldness to her.

He dares to whisper as he stumbles...
'If I can have another chance at it all, things will be different.'

And he whispers again, a little louder...
'If I can have another chance at it all, things will be different.'

Slowly the nightingale and the man in the coarsely woven shirt follow the path that goes up and down, up and down, between the tall trees, until they emerge from the forest. Whilst he has been away his Prime Minister and many others have met and talked and schemed and planned again.

The marksman has been sent for. He has been ordered to shoot upon arrival, the Emperor. So high on top of the palace tower, just as dawn is breaking, the marksman waits. He sees a small bird silhouetted against the crimson sky. Just for the sport of it he takes careful aim, and in that early morning light he shoots the nightingale. The marksman cannot see the Emperor in the shadows, nor would he recognise him in his stable hand's shirt. He congratulates himself on his skill and goes to have a hearty breakfast, boasting of his marksmanship to his friends.

The Emperor, crouched in the shadow of the wall, reaches out. Oh, how he reaches for that silent little bird! He places it so carefully in his pocket, next to his weeping heart. All he wants now is to see his wife. He climbs the walls of the porcelain palace and silently climbs through the large window, into her bedroom. Her chambermaids are sleeping as is the doctor. Her breathing is difficult and strained.

'Hold on, dear one, hold on,' he whispers desperately. 'I will bring you the nightingale's song, hold on.'

Climbing out the window again, he runs along the grand balcony and into the room that was his death chamber. From under the bed he takes out a box, the box of a broken mechanical bird that had once briefly outshone the true nightingale.

All day, hidden in his room, the man in the coarsely woven shirt tries to put the machine bird back together again. With its cogs and its whirrs and its *cluck, cluck, clucks*.

Just before the moon rises he climbs back out the window and runs back along the grand balcony, into the Empress's bedroom. Her breathing is very, very quiet in that now empty, golden room. With shaking hands he winds up the bird that he has so feverishly worked on these past few hours.

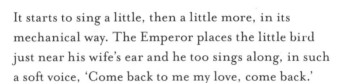

It starts to sing a little, then a little more, in its mechanical way. The Emperor places the little bird just near his wife's ear and he too sings along, in such a soft voice, 'Come back to me my love, come back.'

The Empress opens her eyes. The coldness and indifference that has been between them these past few years has dropped away. She smiles at him and there is a flood of tenderness between them. Her eyes see him and then they stare beyond him and the Emperor softly cries out. Quickly he winds up the bird again. *'Cluck, cluck, cluck, whirr ping,'* sings the bird. *'Cluck, cluck, cluck, whirr ping,'*

'No, no, no,' he softly cries to her. 'No, no, no my love, my life.' She looks at him again, knowing it is the last time she will see her husband's face. And she smiles again and then is gone, beyond him and away.

The man slowly stands and walks along the path, past a little cottage and down to the sea.

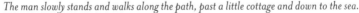

The Emperor places the little bird just near his wife's ear and he too sings along, in such a soft voice . . .

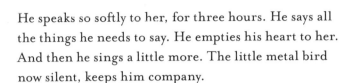

He speaks so softly to her, for three hours. He says all
the things he needs to say. He empties his heart to her.
And then he sings a little more. The little metal bird
now silent, keeps him company.

He hardly remembers the journey back into the forest.
By a small stream he lies and drinks the water. He takes
out the nightingale from his pocket. The bird is stiff
and cold. He washes it in the gentle waters of the stream
and sings to it a little as he digs a little grave. He sings a
little more as he buries the little bird and he imagines
he is burying his wife as well.

He places freshly washed and coloured stones to mark
the place. He sings a little more and a little more. Then
he drinks once more from the stream. As he looks up
there is a great stag standing near him, watching him
with its large, dark eyes. And the many deer are
standing still, right next to the stag. They all look on
this man, and they wonder in him.

The man slowly stands and walks along the path, past a
little cottage and down to the sea. And the stag and the
deer follow him.

As the days and weeks and months pass, even though he
is filled with grief, there is also something new.

Down by the sea, he sings again. The gulls call out to
him as he sings and the fishermen come in from their
boats to the shore. The singing reminds them of things
past, and people past, and things that have happened
long ago. Sometimes the man visits the little cottage that
belongs to the maid of the kitchen and her mother. He
sings to them but he leaves the door open so that others
passing by can hear too.